Finding
HAPPY

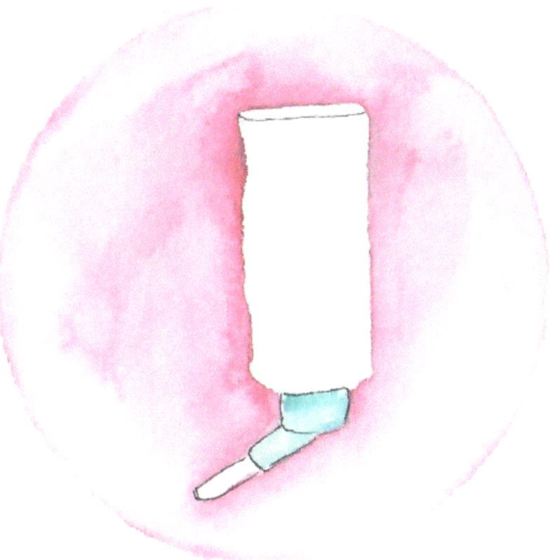

Written and Illustrated by

KRISTEN L. SCHINDLER

Published by Pen It! Publications, LLC in the U.S.A.

812-371-4128 www.penitpublications.com

ISBN: 978-1-63984-225-4

Illustrated by Author

Please scan the following QR code with your phone's camera function to take you directly to https://kristenleeschindler.com/finding-happy-book . Once there you will see a link to listen to the full "Finding Happy" audiobook narrated by me personally. I have found, as a mother of three children who all struggled with reading in various ways, that listening to audiobooks while following along with the printed text is a great way for children to access new vocabulary and build their confidence with their own reading skills. Although nothing compares to them having 'lap time' with loved ones reading to them and modeling strong reading skills, also having access to audio is a great way to set up reading stations in classrooms or at home. Happy listening and reading!

Dedication

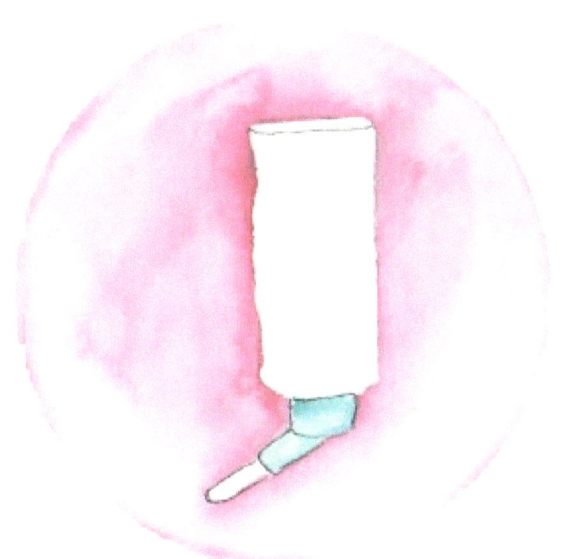 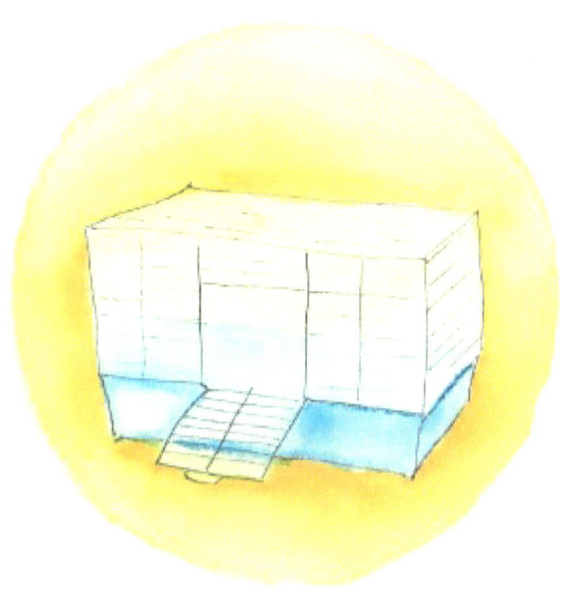 

To Gavin, Logan, and Ava

May you always find the Happy that
resides in your heart. Never forget
to surround yourselves with love,
laughter, and the beauty of this world.

There once was a little girl
named Lilly Anna Grace.
She was always filled with energy
and had a smile upon her face.

She bounced and jumped,
she ran and skipped.
Her heart was filled with joy.
Sticks and rocks became creations.
She barely played with toys.

Nature was her wonderland.
She filled her time in trees.
She frolicked in the water and
conversed with honey bees.

For her seventh birthday,
she asked for something new.
It was a lively little puppy that
she had dreamed about, too.

In her mind she saw it clearly,

with big brown eyes and soft, white fluff.

She would train it, love it,

snuggle it, and do all kinds of stuff.

Her parents slightly disagreed.
They said she wasn't ready yet,
for such a big responsibility.
Maybe a smaller pet.

They suggested perhaps some fish,
That would swim and dive and glow.
But she couldn't snuggle a fish.
So, she said, "No, I don't think so."

She hung her head quite sadly,

while trying to think of something new.

Then her dad suggested a guinea pig,

"They are cute, sweet, and fun, too!"

"What's a guinea pig?" Lilly Anna Grace questioned.

"What can I do with a pet like that?

Are they pink?

Do they stink?

Do they grunt and get really fat?"

Her parents laughed and giggled.

"No, you silly girl.

A guinea pig is soft and sweet.

Let's give the idea a whirl."

They ventured to a pet store
where in a cage one sat.
It was small and fluffy.
It was tiny and not fat.

When Lilly Anna Grace saw it's tiny little face,
she knew right away this was the place.
Her heart began to flutter and simultaneously melt.
She remembered her dream and this was how it felt.

When she finally got to hold it,

it was so soft and smooth and sleek.

With light brown fur and dark black eyes.

It was quite small, quiet and sweet.

"She's just perfect for me!" Lilly Anna Grace
exclaimed. "Can I please take her home?

I will be a perfect pig mom,

and I will never let her roam."

So, they packed up her gift with hay and pebbles, too.

A new pig cage, a water bottle, and a snuggle hut, all new.

The pig was very tiny.

She was much different from the rest.

And when Lilly held her,

the pig snuggled gently on her chest.

"I need the perfect name for my precious little pet.

It needs to be very special, but I can't think of one just yet."

"Well, take your time, our sweet, sweet girl.

Just you wait and see.

Go show her the beautiful flowers,

and where you love to be."

So, off they went, pig and girl.

Each day was big and new.

There were so many sights to see.

There were so many fun things to do.

But, sometimes pig got squealy,

like she was trying to say a word.

Although their language was different,

Lilly Anna Grace was sure she heard.

"Don't be afraid, my small sweet pig.

there is nothing to fear.

I will always protect you.

I will always be near."

It seemed the pig, she understood
the words from this sweet girl.
So, pig did a happy popcorn dance
And the girl began to twirl.

They danced and popped,
They jumped and hopped.
Together they explored and played.
And when their bodies got too tired,
they stopped and upon
the ground they laid.

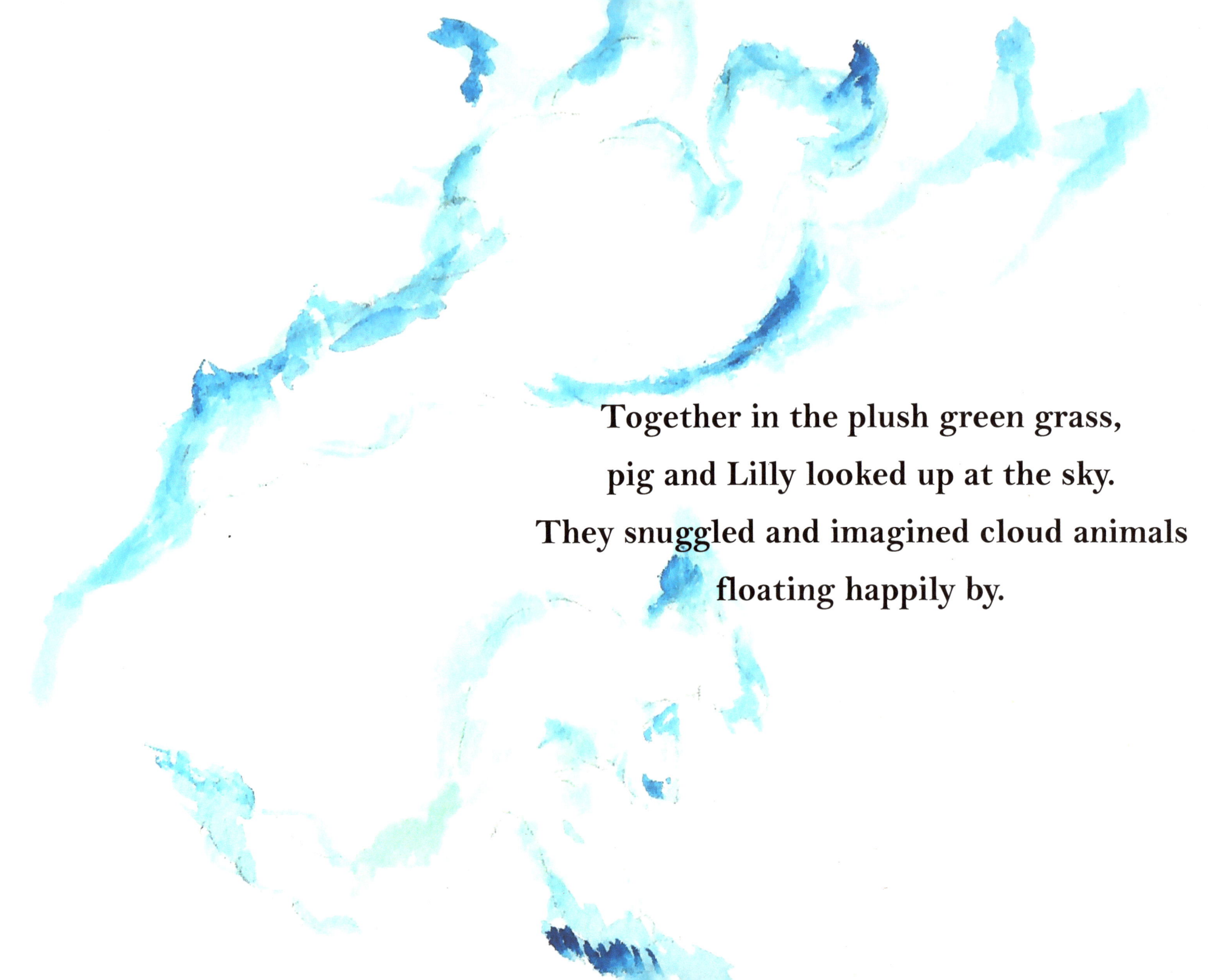

Together in the plush green grass,

pig and Lilly looked up at the sky.

They snuggled and imagined cloud animals

floating happily by.

Together they saw fierce dragons,
long-tailed parrots, and momma kangaroos.
They saw tiny dogs, jumping frogs,
and giant antlered moose.

Then Lilly turned to pig and said,

"I need a name for you,

but nothing seems just right.

I try to think of names in the morning

and then again at night."

The pig looked up like she was thinking too.

This sweet, sweet girl was her world.

What could a small pig do?

So, pig did what happy pigs do,

she hopped and popped galore.

She ran up to Lilly; she jumped again,

and she did it more and more.

Lilly laughed and giggled.

"Pig, you are so cuddly and happy.

You always make my day!

I can't imagine spending time doing what I love,

in any other way."

"That's it!" Lilly squealed.

"Why didn't I think of it before?

I've found the perfect fit for you!

You will be HAPPY,

From today and forever more."

So, Happy and Lilly headed home,

to snuggle down and rest up from their long first week.

For tomorrow would bring

more adventures,

more hops,

more pops,

and squeaks.

The End

Guinea Pig Research

Do you have questions about guinea pigs? Do you wonder where they live and what they eat? Having questions is a great place to start.

When my children wanted a guinea pig, we went to the library to learn more about them. We checked out books about guinea pigs, we watched video about them, and even went to the St. Louis Zoo to visit an exhibit to ask the zookeepers our questions. Then we designed and built a habitat for our guineas, so they could have enough room to popcorn, hop, and wear unicorn horns!

You can become a guinea pig expert, too! Or maybe you have another animal you are interested in learning about. Your brain is so talented and there is so much information out there. The most important part is to have fun, work hard, and be creative. Then tell your story of what you have learned so you can inspire others along the way!

Author Kristen Lee Schindler is a homeschooling mom of three, author of two books, "All the Things" and "Finding Happy". She is also a Podcast host of "All the Things with Kristen Schindler", a personal coach, a business broker, and an international missionary currently doing work in the country of Sri Lanka.

Kristen spent over 23 years in the public and private world of education teaching in various capacities with a focus on Language Arts and helping her students find their voices. For the last four years, she has enjoyed pouring into her own children as her family continues their journey of homeschooling and sharing her voice with her readers.

Kristen has always loved to listen to other people's stories and share her story with others. Her mission is to show up each day authentically, vulnerably, and listen to the hearts of others. With navigating the ins and outs of over eighteen years of both parenting and working, she is keenly aware of the delicate and challenging need of keeping "All the T.H.I.N.G.S." in balance. She has felt called to share how together we can lift each other up to do that well. She longs to help people "Show Up Strong" for themselves, those they love, and those they are called to serve.

Kristen loves to see the connections and richness that communication and an openness to others hearts and experiences brings to the fabric of our lives. She is continually reminded that despite her desire to keep a firm grasp on all the things she would like to control, God has positioned himself to do the driving of her life. She is merely a passenger. Her children have always loved animals, but this book was inspired by the real-life love between her daughter, Ava, and her sweet guinea pig, Chloe. She was one of the sweetest pigs who loved grapes, snuggling, reading books, and playing pool.

This book is based on the true-life love affair between my daughter, Ava, and her sweet guinea pig, Chloe, who loved snuggling, playing pool, eating grapes, and wearing unicorn horns.